LIFE IS NO FAIR!

by Stephen Manes

illustrated by Warren Miller

E. P. DUTTON · NEW YORK

Library of Congress Cataloging in Publication Data
Manes, Stephen, date
  Life is no fair!
  Summary: Humorous anecdotes portray the injustices
of life.
    1.Wit and humor, Juvenile.   [1. Life—Anecdotes,
facetiae, satire, etc.   2. Justice—Anecdotes, facetiae,
satire, etc.]   I. Miller, Warren, date   ill.
II. Title.
PN6163.M26   1985   818'.5402   84-21095
ISBN 0-525-44192-1

Published in the United States by E. P. Dutton, Inc.,
2 Park Avenue, New York, N.Y. 10016
Published simultaneously in Canada by
Fitzhenry & Whiteside Limited, Toronto
Editor: Ann Durell   Designer: Edith T. Weinberg
Printed in Hong Kong by South China Printing Co.
First Edition   COBE   10 9 8 7 6 5 4 3 2 1

for Carolyn
S.M.

to Anna, Daniel, and Sarah
W.M.

When his family moved away from the old
neighborhood, Willard Twombley worried that
he'd never make another friend.

He never did.

Brunhilde Dalrymple was afraid that if she turned out the lights, some horrible four-armed creature with long fangs and a slimy body might slither through the night and carry her away.

Actually, the creature had only three arms.

When Bronislaw Babushka refused to eat his
vegetables, his parents told him he'd never grow
up big and strong.

They were half right.

"You can't possibly fall off," Mrs. Wimple
told her son Orville when they first set foot on
the observation deck of the world's tallest building.
"It's ridiculous to be afraid of heights."

Orville was not convinced.

"There is no such thing as a flying saucer!"
Professor Chuzzlewit told his morning astronomy
class.

He wasn't wrong.

"What do you mean things could be worse?"
moaned Hildegarde Bernstein to her husband as
they stood knee-deep in muck, trying to push their
brand-new Schnauzenheim-Fogel out of the Great
Dismal Swamp. "How could things possibly be
worse?"

She found out.

"There's something funny about this place," astronaut Lydia Pinkwater radioed home from the planet Blilb.

It wasn't as funny as she thought.

When Hugo Normous refused to quit picking on him, Tiny Teedle decided he had only two choices: to run or to fight.

He picked the wrong one.

Lance Allot was a handsome movie star. He had eight expensive cars, three huge yachts, six of the world's largest mansions, and twelve million dollars in the bank. But was he truly happy?

You bet!

At breakfast, George Gorge had fourteen hard-boiled eggs, fifteen hamburgers, sixteen pancakes, seventeen plates of french-fried onion rings, eighteen pieces of boysenberry pie, and a glass of milk.

At lunch, George decided to stop drinking milk because it gave him indigestion.

A friendly witch told Princess Cynthia
Ogle-Smythe III that if she kissed a certain
enchanted frog, it would turn into a handsome
prince.

The witch was misinformed.

"All right, I give up," said Herman to Sherman. "What has eight wings, six legs, four eyes, and a two-foot stinger?"

"Beats me," said Sherman.

Cranshaw Coconino absolutely refused to get his
hair cut.

At the age of twenty-two, he was voted most popular monster in the history of the movies.

While her brother worked sixteen-hour days at the grit factory, Wilhelmina Sloath lay on her sofa, munched one-pound bags of potato chips, watched people win huge prizes on television game shows, and sighed "Life is no fair."

How right she was!